THE
Little
Witch

Written by **Michael Pellico**

Illustrated by Christina Berry

See more children's books by Moonbow Publishing at:

https://MoonbowPublishing.com

Second Print Edition
ISBN 978-1-7339130-7-2
Library of Congress Control Number: 2020916935
Printed in USA

This book is dedicated to:
Sabrina Pellico
The inspiration for this story...
and many others.

And to my mother:
Helen Pellico
My hero and guiding light
throughout my life.

It was Halloween and there was a spooky stillness in the air as the sun began to set over the valley. The sky and all that the light touched glowed pumpkin-orange. For Sabrina and her brother Stephen, it had been a wonderful day. They got to wear their costumes to school and were just about finished with trick-or-treating in their neighborhood.

As the two passed by the open meadow at the end of their street, they noticed a crowd of children standing around the old beech tree where they liked to play. The kids were talking excitedly and looking up at the tree.

When they approached, Sabrina asked "What's going on here?"

The children pointed and shouted: "Look! There's a witch up there! She can't get away because she dropped her broom!"

3

Stephen was skeptical, "How do you know she is a real witch and not just in a costume?" The boys told the brother and sister that they saw her fly and crash into the tree, dropping her broom.

Sabrina looked closely at the tree, examining the place where the leaves had been disturbed from the crash. There sitting on a branch high up in the tree was a little witch! She looked to be about the same age. The little witch did not look scary but very nervous. Sabrina turned to the children and asked, "Has anyone tried to talk to her?"

"Oh no" the boys replied, "we just want to catch her. Witches are bad!"

Sabrina remembered a time in her life when she had felt scared and misunderstood and in need of a friend. She picked up the broom and told the children, "I am going to climb up the tree and give the broom back to her. She is little and seems afraid of us!"

The children cried out: "No, no, you can't trust a witch! Once she has her magic broom back, she will do something bad to us!"

Then Stephen spoke up: "My sister is right, we should treat others how we would like to be treated and help her."

Luckily, growing up with an older brother and many rowdy boys in her neighborhood, Sabrina was an excellent climber. She used her strength to pull herself up to the tree branch opposite the little witch. "Here, I brought you the broom you dropped" she said catching her breath. "May I sit here for a minute with you?"

The little witch was timid at first, but seeing Sabrina's bright smile made her expression soften. "Yes, you may," the little witch said with a shy smile, "Thank you for giving my broom back to me."

"You're welcome! My name is Sabrina. What is yours?"

"My name is Anna."

"How old are you?" Sabrina asked, "I am seven."

The little witch said, "I am seven too...
at least I think so. I am not sure because
witches do not celebrate birthdays."

"No birthdays? But that means no
birthday parties! Birthdays are so much
fun...with cake, ice cream, games and lots
of presents."

The little witch looked down and seemed sad. "That does sound like fun. I wish I had a birthday party. Mostly because I wish I had friends... but everyone seems to be afraid of witches."

Sabrina took the little witch's hand and said, "You can be my friend and we will have a big party for you!"

The little witch's face brightened with a smile, "Really? You will be my friend?"

"Of course I will be your friend and I will invite my friends too! I am sure they will like you!"

Sabrina glanced toward the ground, remembering her brother and noticing the blue of the night creeping in.

"I better get back down there. It is getting dark and my parents will be expecting me home soon."

"I must leave too," said Anna, "I am very happy we met. I hope we can play together another time."

"Of course we can, anytime you like! I live right over there" Sabrina pointed. "Just be careful with your landing!"

"I will!" They both laughed.

When Sabrina got to the ground, the children had many questions for her:

"What happened?"

"Did she hurt you?"

"No, she was very nice and we are now friends," she said.

"We do not believe you! She is a witch!"

Just then, there was a rustling sound in the tree. Suddenly, the little witch blasted out from the leaves on her broomstick. Above them she circled the tree several times. The little witch spoke some magic words and waved her hand over the tree.

The boys cried out, "Oh no, she is a bad witch! She's going to put a spell on us!"

The leaves on the tree began to shake wildly as if they were dancing. The children couldn't believe their eyes as they watched the leaves transform into all different kinds of candy and fall to the ground. They leapt with joy and laughter as the candy rained gently down on them. They grabbed handfuls of it and filled their trick-or-treat bags.

The little witch circled around again one
last time to say goodbye to Sabrina.

"You have shown me great kindness
instead of fear and judgment. You tried
to understand me and how I was feeling.
You've made this day a happy one I'll
always remember and now I have a real
friend."

They waved to each other and the little
witch disappeared into the beautiful
Halloween night sky.

The End

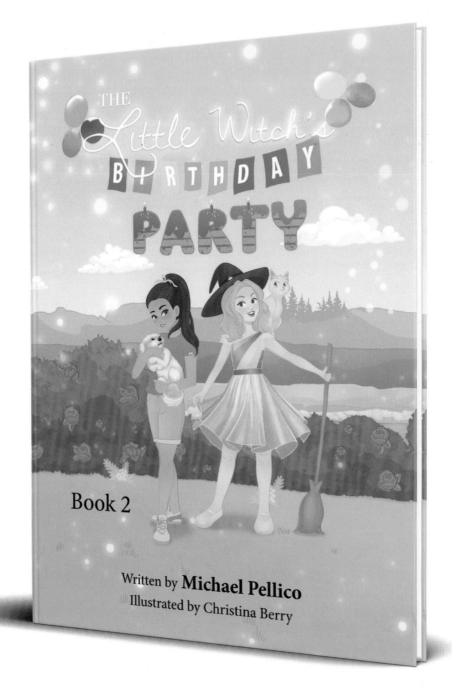

Find out how the birthday party for the little witch turns out in Book 2: The Little Witch's Birthday Party available at MoonbowPublishing.com

About the Author

Michael Pellico is a medical researcher, writer, and film producer. One of eleven children whose parents both worked long hours. It was his responsibility to help raise his siblings. Growing up "poor", he entertained them with stories, and later telling stories to their children. This book and all his stories are dedicated to Sabrina, his niece, who insists that he tell her a story each time they are together. We hope that you love them as much as Sabrina does!

About the Illustrator

Christina Berry is an established book artist who enjoys all types of mediums in illustration. She has spent much of her adult life pursuing a degree in Microbiology and working with special needs kids, but she changed course to her first love; art. Christina works from home in Los Angeles, California and loves to foster and rescue cats.

Check out the other great titles at: MoonbowPublishing.com